SPEED RACER

The Official Racing Book

PRICE STERN SLOAN
Published by the Penguin Group
Penguin Group (USA) Inc., 375 Hudson Street,
New York, New York 10014, USA
Penguin Group (Canada), 90 Eglinton Avenue East, Suite 700, Toronto, Ontario M4P 2Y3, Canada
(a division of Pearson Penguin Canada Inc.)
Penguin Books Ltd., 80 Strand, London WC2R 0RL, England
Penguin Group Ireland, 25 St. Stephen's Green, Dublin 2, Ireland
(a division of Penguin Books Ltd.)
Penguin Group (Australia), 250 Camberwell Road, Camberwell, Victoria 3124, Australia
(a division of Pearson Australia Group Pty. Ltd.)
Penguin Books India Pvt. Ltd., 11 Community Centre, Panchsheel Park, New Delhi—110 017, India
Penguin Group (NZ), 67 Apollo Drive, Rosedale, North Shore 0632, New Zealand
(a division of Pearson New Zealand Ltd.)
Penguin Books (South Africa) (Pty.) Ltd., 24 Sturdee Avenue, Rosebank, Johannesburg 2196, South Africa

Penguin Books Ltd., Registered Offices:
80 Strand, London WC2R 0RL, England

www.speedracerthemovie.com

The publisher does not have any control over and does not assume any responsibility
for author or third-party websites or their content.

ISBN 978-0-8431-3207-6   10 9 8 7 6 5 4 3 2 1

SPEED RACER

The Official Racing Book

By Sophia Kelly
Based upon the film *Speed Racer* written and directed
by the Wachowski brothers.

PSS!
PRICE STERN SLOAN

Racing fans, this is the book you've been waiting for all season!

Inside this Official Racing Book you'll find tons of information about some of the greatest winners and most notorious losers that ever zoomed down a World Racing League (WRL) track, as well as facts and figures about the fast-paced, high-stakes world of auto racing. This is a car-centric culture where racing isn't just a sport—it's a way of life. Each car is like a beautiful piece of art unique to its owner and reflective of the driver's personality. Race cars are capable of speeds in excess of four hundred miles per hour. Who can resist cheering as these cars drift their way through some of the toughest turns and steepest drops in the world?

Sit back and enjoy the ride!

Table of Contents

RACER MOTORS

Meet the Racer Motors Team

Speed Racer

Speed Racer grew up breathing, eating, and sleeping auto racing. The sky's the limit when it comes to the feats of his career.

"Racing is in our blood."
—Speed Racer

The brains of the operation, Pops Racer, is perhaps the greatest auto engineer on the planet. After all, he's the man who designed the Mach 5. This former wrestler loves to tackle any challenge.

"My sons are the most important things I've ever done in my life."
—Pops Racer

Pops Racer

Mom Racer

Mom Racer is always ready to inspire her family with a kind word and a loving embrace. She's the loudest cheerer in any grandstand.

"We just have to stick together."
—Mom Racer

Chim-Chim is Spritle's best friend and always at the ready with a monkey cookie whenever the need arises!

Chim-Chim

He's more than just the Racer Motors mechanic—he's part of the Racer family. Sparky is indispensable during races, giving Speed advice and encouragement through his headset.

"Holy cannoli, Speed!"
—Sparky

Trixie

Trixie can often be found hovering in the skies in the TRX, her pink and black helicopter, keeping an eye on her number one man, Speed Racer.

"Cool beans!"
—Trixie

Spritle is the youngest and most mischievous of the Racer family. There's no racing fact or figure that Spritle Racer doesn't know. Will he be the next star in the Racer family?

"I think I know just how to help!"
—Spritle Racer

Spritle Racer

Go, Speed Racer, Go!

After years of racing, Speed Racer has emerged as a real competitor in the World Racing League. The son of the famous auto engineer, Pops Racer, and the brother of the former racing star, Rex Racer, Speed was born in the driver's seat. This year he's out to prove that he's a force to be reckoned with.

But it's not only Speed's ability on the track that makes him such a gigantic figure in today's racing world. Speed Racer remains one of the few independent racers in the WRL—he does not have any sponsors—and races on his father's team, Racer Motors.

"No one seems able to lay a glove on this kid!"
—Thunderhead Raceway announcer

Growing Up Racer

By Chrissy Hood

Speed Racer's performance this year on the WRL circuit has been phenomenal. One question has been on everyone's mind—how does he do it? One thing's for sure—Speed's heart beats for racing. This reporter believes that this passion might have a little something to do with his childhood—growing up Racer.

Speed Racer was born into the legendary Racer family. His father, Pops Racer, was once a top engineer for the famous Mishida Motorwerks, where he designed some of the world's best race cars. Pops Racer quit his job to open his own company, Racer Motors. It was there that Pops designed the legendary Mach 5—possibly the most genius car ever made.

But it's not just the Mach 5 that makes Speed the best driver in the world. It's also the initial training he received from his talented and often controversial brother, Rex Racer. When Speed was a child, Rex would take him to the Thunderhead Raceway to teach him all about the art of driving a race car. Speed lived for racing since the day he could walk. In fact, Speed learned to drive before he could walk. He lost his two front teeth in his first crash while he was practicing driving with Rex in the Mach 4. His mother even told us in a candid interview that, "Before he could even talk, Speed was making noises that sounded like a car engine."

But for some, Speed's career is overshadowed by Rex's questionable legacy. Once a promising young driver on the Racer Motors team, Rex set the course record at the Thunderhead Raceway behind the wheel of the Mach 4. It seemed as though he was poised for a career filled with unbelievable success. But things aren't always as they seem. Not long after that heroic night at Thunderhead, Rex Racer quit his family's team to race for other teams on the WRL circuit. Some say that he nearly ruined racing, while others claim that he single-handedly tried to save the sport from the corporate sponsors. Some say he took out dirty racers who worked for one of racing's major corporations, while others claim that he took orders from the criminal underworld.

Was Rex Racer a hero or a villain? The world may never know. Nearly a decade ago, Rex died when he crashed in the Maltese Ice Caves during the Casa Cristo 5000 and his kwik-save foam failed to activate.

Despite the controversy surrounding Rex's life and death, all signs point to a long and fruitful career ahead for Speed Racer. Will anyone ever beat this talented driver? Who knows? Maybe when he's old enough, Speed's younger brother, Spritle, will join the family business. Just imagine how packed the grandstands would be if two Racers went head-to-head.

"Before he could even talk,
        Speed was making noises
that sounded like a car engine."
                                —Mom Racer

The Genius of the Mach 5

The Mach 5 is Speed's everyday car—he uses it on the street and in rally races. Designed by world-class engineer Pops Racer, the Mach 5 got a little boost from Racer X's mechanic Minx before the Casa Cristo 5000 this year. It seems that Speed Racer can do anything with a push of one of the buttons on the steering wheel. Check them out!

Button A releases a set of hydraulic jump-jacks. These jump-jacks can be used to jump over anything blocking the Mach 5's path.

Button B seals the cockpit, creating a bulletproof barrier between Speed and any dirty racers that are out to get him.

Button C activates tire shields so that no illegal tire shanks can throw the Mach 5 out of the running.

Button D inflates a Hexa-Dyno emergency spare tire. In the event that something damages the Mach 5's tires, Speed can get back in the race without missing a beat.

Button E activates Zircon-tipped saw blades out from the front of the car. These powerful saws can cut through almost anything. They're the perfect tool for off-road driving.

Button F projects tire crampons that help the Mach 5 maneuver through any road conditions, including ice!

Button G launches a remote control homing bird that can transmit UCAP footage from anywhere, to anywhere. This way, if Speed is in trouble, he can always find help.

The Marvelous Mach 6

When Speed's roaring down the racetrack, it's the Mach 6 that takes him from start to finish. Check it out!

Life in the Pit Crew

By Stan Pitt

Think life in the pit crew is the pits? Think again! This reporter had the privilege of spending a day shadowing Speed Racer's right-hand man and Pops Racer's MVP—Sparky! This talented mechanic not only works magic on the Mach 5 and the Mach 6, he's also Speed's guardian angel on the racetrack, warning him if a driver is coming up too close and giving advice on how to handle the rocky road ahead. He's even been known to calm down the superstar driver just before a big race!

Talk to Sparky for five minutes, and you'll quickly realize that there are no two people he admires more than Pops and Speed Racer. So if it's life in the fast lane you're looking for, look no farther than the pit crew. Sparky's on fire!

The Harbinger of Boom

He's known as the Harbinger of Boom. Others call him Racer Hex or the Masked Racer. Around the track, he's known as Racer X. Many mysteries surround him. Who is he? Whose side is he on? Where did he come from? What does he look like behind that mask? Is he a headhunter or one of the best racers on the WRL circuit today? One thing's for sure: Whoever you are Racer X, you certainly make the world of racing a more interesting place to live. Don't ever hit the brakes!

"He drives like he's not always interested in winning."

—Five-time Casa Cristo champion, Johnny "Good Boy" Jones

Racer X's X-treme Cars

Whether he's on the street or on the racetrack, Racer X's cars are always ahead of the pack! Check them out!

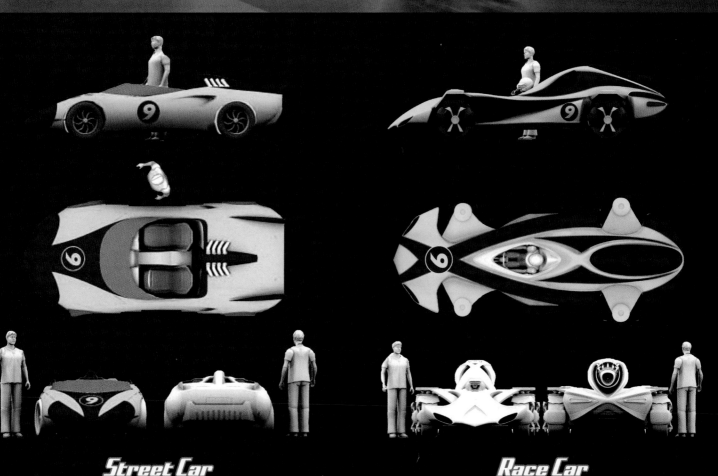

Street Car

Race Car

The Royal Treatment

By Ace Grill

This reporter got a VIP tour of internationally-renowned racing sponsor Royalton Industries, where cars are built and racers are made! And let me be the first to tell you that this facility is truly out of this world!

I got my first stunning impression of Royalton Tower when I entered the Royalton Car Museum, which houses some of the greatest cars ever to grace a WRL track, including the Crystal Horse with the Apache Super-Charger—the car that won the '69, '70, and '72 Grand Prixs!

As if that weren't awe-inspiring enough, I was then taken to the modern T-180 factory, a vertically-integrated plant where workers and machines can build one of these amazing cars from scratch in only thirty-six hours! This factory is also where the Royalton engineers create the world-class engines that go into a Royalton race car. This facility boasts the only transponder foundry in the world, outside of Musha Motors.

Next, I visited the Team Royalton training facility, where some of the most famous race car drivers in the world get into top physical shape. This state-of-the-art facility is not just a gym. It also provides instruction on martial arts and gymnastics, as well as energy-resistance training. Race car drivers always need to be in perfect physical condition whenever they step on the gas pedal—after all, drivers must be able to withstand over 4 g's of force in a typical race.

The last stop on my tour was the luxurious Drivers' Club, where the Royalton race car drivers go to unwind after a long day of practicing or a draining race. There's a full maid service, a personal chef, and a masseuse available 24/7. The Royalton race car drivers might work hard, but they play hard, too!

So, the next time you find yourself in Cosmopolis, make sure to catch a tour of Royalton Tower. It's guaranteed to *drive* you wild!

WRL Drivers

SNAKE OILER

Who's that in the orange and black car? It's Snake Oiler—leader of the Hydra-Cell Racing Team. Watch out for him on the racetrack!

Gray Ghost

If you're watching Gray Ghost on the racetrack, you'd better watch closely—he earned his nickname due to his signature move, weaving in and out of his competitors' sightlines. Even the spectacular Speed Racer has been outraced by Gray Ghost's skillful driving. But Speed Racer doesn't have any hard feelings about that. No matter who wins, racing against this talented and honorable driver puts the fun and spirit back in auto racing.

Jack "Cannonball" Taylor

Jack "Cannonball" Taylor is considered one of the greatest drivers ever to place a wheel on a racetrack. A star racer for Royalton Industries, Cannonball is a two-time Grand Prix winner and five-time World Racing League champion. Destined to hold a top position in the WRL Hall of Fame, he is the hero of every little boy and girl who loves auto racing.

Lightning Strikes Twice
at the Thunderhead Raceway

The audience watched in awe as Speed Racer tore up the track at the Thunderhead Raceway. No one had seen moves like that since Rex Racer, driving the Mach 4, set the record at the track eight years ago.

It was obvious as soon as the Mach 6 tore away from the starting line that this was Speed Racer's night. Drivers who tried to get in Speed's way simply got put in their place—last place, that is. But it was almost as if Speed wasn't alone in the lead. He seemed to be chasing someone— the ghost of Rex Racer. It looked as though Speed might even beat his brother's record, but Speed came in a second too late. And Rex's record still stands at Thunderhead!

"Speed Racer is just gobbling up this track!"

—Thunderhead Raceway announcer

Built across an archipelago and set against the glittering sea, Fuji Helexicon is one of the most beautiful settings for the WRL. This exciting racetrack weaves in and out of the tropical landscape with its gravity-defying twists and turns. This track will test the bravery of even the most skilled driver.

Welcome to the
Casa Cristo 5000

Known as the "grand dame of cross-country racing,"
the Casa Cristo 5000 is the second oldest rally race
in the world, spanning two continents, three climate
changes, and five thousand kilometers of some of the
most winding and treacherous roads ever raced.

The race starts when the Queen of Casa Cristo sees
the sun and signals to the racers. The drivers race in
street cars, rather than race cars, on this cross-country
road rally. More than going fast, the race is about
endurance. Winning Casa Cristo is a test of will.

The winner of the Casa Cristo road rally is
automatically offered an invitation to the Grand Prix.

"Casa Cristo isn't just
about going fast . . .
It's about endurance."

Key Competitors

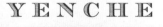

Yen Che: You can't miss this unbelievable team, with dynamic moves and unstoppable energy. Watch out for their exploding tires!

Flying Foxes Freight: Watch out for this super-sly, super-fly team, led by the foxiest driver around, Delila! But don't let them get too close or you may find a tire shank piercing your tire!

Hydra-Cell: Led by the infamous Snake Oiler, this team is poised to be the front-runner at this year's rally. This team always has something up its sleeve . . .

Thor-Axine Inc.: These drivers from the north are here to heat things up! There's a reason their cars are shaped like Norse hammers!

Togokahn Motors: Led by Taejo Togokahn, this wildcard team includes the young rising star Speed Racer and the mysterious Racer X.

Here's what you can expect from this incredibly challenging course:

DAY 1:

By Arthur Truck

This year's 82nd annual road rally will start out with what many people consider the hardest part of the race—the forest of arches and columns that makes up the Muqranna. Cars must weave through a series of columns to successfully continue the race. Just this first section alone has proven too much for some racers, who have crashed and tumbled over each other in this maze.

The racers who make it through emerge onto the Casa Cristo Cliff and then into the sandstorm of the Zunubian desert. But drivers had better watch out! Race officials have done a great job cleaning up the dirty tricks in this rally race over the years, but there are always a few bad eggs who give this race its nickname, the Crucible. All the teams will need to bring their very best just to finish the first day of the race.

DAY 2:

Day 2 always proves to be as high-octane as the day before. Teams have to close any gaps between themselves and the leaders as they swerve through the tight mountain roads. If they manage to make it through, they'll head right into the Maltese Ice Caves. Only the most masterful drivers will negotiate the dangerous "S" curves with any speed and make it out the other side. These caves have marked the end of the race for many drivers, but surviving the Maltese Ice Caves is not the final obstacle! Drivers must still navigate the treacherous roads all the way to the finish line.

Count the number of teams who make it through this final leg—it's usually a lot lower than the number of teams who started the race. Why would so many teams set out on this dangerous quest knowing that the odds were stacked against them? Because the winner of the Casa Cristo receives the last remaining slot for the Grand Prix, and that's a prize that money can't buy.

"First rule of rally racing: If you aren't cheating, you aren't trying."

—Taejo Togokahn

Key Competitors

Prince Kabala

Nitro Venderhoss

Ekpyrosis

Kellie Kalinkov

КРЫША КОРПОРАЦИЯ

The Greatest Grand Prix

The Grand Prix is the pinnacle of the WRL and takes place in the amazing Grand Prix Coliseum in the heart of Cosmopolis. This race is so renowned that it is called by announcers from all over the world and broadcast in more than 80 languages. The towering grandstands rise up among the city's skyscrapers and the track itself is so intricate that it looks as if it were made of origami with cloverleaf formations and gravity-defying drops.

WRL Facts and Figures

- The Casa Cristo 5000 is the second oldest rally race in the world, spanning two continents, three climate changes, and five thousand kilometers of some of the most winding and treacherous roads ever raced. It's such a brutal test of endurance that its nickname is the Crucible.

- Prince Kabala's jewel-encrusted race car is worth an estimated $22 million.

- The engineers at the T-180 factory at Royalton Industries can build a T-180, from initial carbon bond to finished car, in only thirty-six hours.

- The best T-180 drivers must be able to withstand over 4 g's of force in a typical race.

- The Vundervopper with the K-9 twin-turbine won the Grand Prix in '71. The Crystal Horse with the Apache Super-Charger won the Grand Prix in '69, '70, and '72. The Kenobe Motorstar rebuilt with a VC triple chamber won the Grand Prix in '73.

- Speed Racer wears his lucky red socks to every race. Rex Racer used to do the same thing. Both brothers believed it brings good luck out on the racetrack.

- Rex Racer still holds the record at the Thunderhead Raceway.

- Legend has it that Ben Burns drove the last lap of the '68 Vanderbilt Cup with his eyes closed.

- First-place drivers celebrate their victory with an ice-cold jug of milk.